P9-CLF-614

Wytheville Public Library

WITHDRAWN

FEB 2 0 2007

WITHDRAWN

Firefighters in the Dark

WITHDRAWN
63 East Genesee Street
Baldwinsville, NY 13027-2575

TO MY PARENTS,
who encouraged me to imagine—D.S.

TO EVA,
my colorful friend and an amazing storyteller—N.C.

Copyright © 2006 by Dashka Slater
Illustrations copyright © 2006 by Nicoletta Ceccoli

All rights reserved. For information about permission to reproduce selections from this book,
write to Permissions, Houghton Mifflin Company, 215 Park Avenue South, New York, New York 10003.
www.houghtonmifflinbooks.com

The text of this book is set in Triplex Serif Light.
The illustrations are done using acrylics and pastels.
Book design by Carol Goldenberg

Library of Congress Cataloging-in-Publication Data

Slater, Dashka.
Firefighters in the dark / by Dashka Slater ; illustrated by Nicoletta Ceccoli.
p. cm.
Summary: While in bed at night, an imaginative child hears sirens from the nearby fire station
and creates fantastic stories about what the firefighters are going to do.
ISBN 0-618-55459-9 (hardcover)
[1. Firefighters—Fiction. 2. Imagination—Fiction.] I. Ceccoli, Nicoletta, ill. II. Title.
PZ7.S62897Fi 2006
[E]—dc22
2005003915
ISBN-13: 978-0-618-55459-1

Manufactured in China
SCP 10 9 8 7 6 5 4 3 2 1

Firefighters in the Dark

by Dashka Slater

illustrated by Nicoletta Ceccoli

Houghton Mifflin Company ◗ Boston 2006

The fire station is near my house.
At night, I can hear the sirens howling.
I'm in my bed, and my eyes are closed,
but I listen,
and I know where they are going.

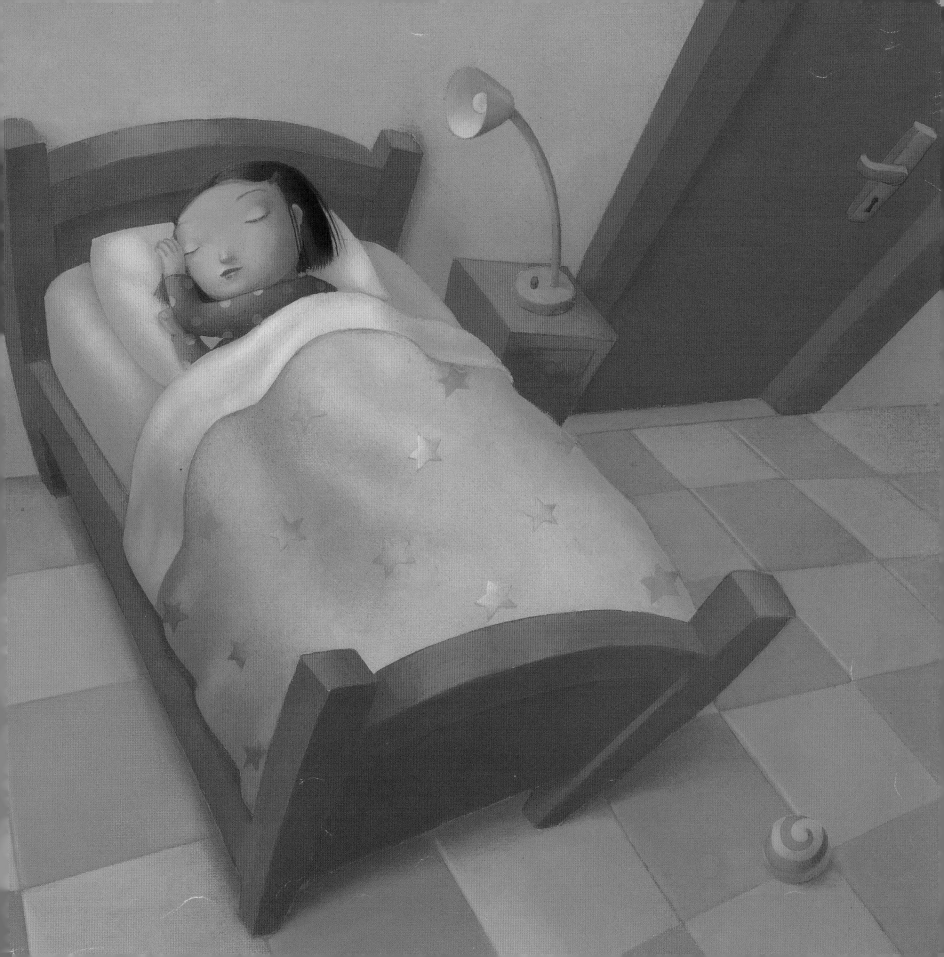

Tonight, there's a castle on fire.
The knights are running around like crazy,
and the king and the queen and the fifteen little princesses
are all screaming, "Help, firefighters! Help!"

What happened was this:
A fire-breathing dragon stopped in for dinner
and his potatoes were too hot.
He blew on them to cool them off
and set the table on fire.

Luckily, the firefighters are close by.
They chop down the roof of the castle with their axes,
and the pumper truck pumps water from the moat.

Pretty soon, the fire is out.
The fifteen baby princesses go back to playing hide-and-seek
and the knights go riding off on their horses
to tell the dragon that next time he can have only cold things to eat,
like Popsicles.

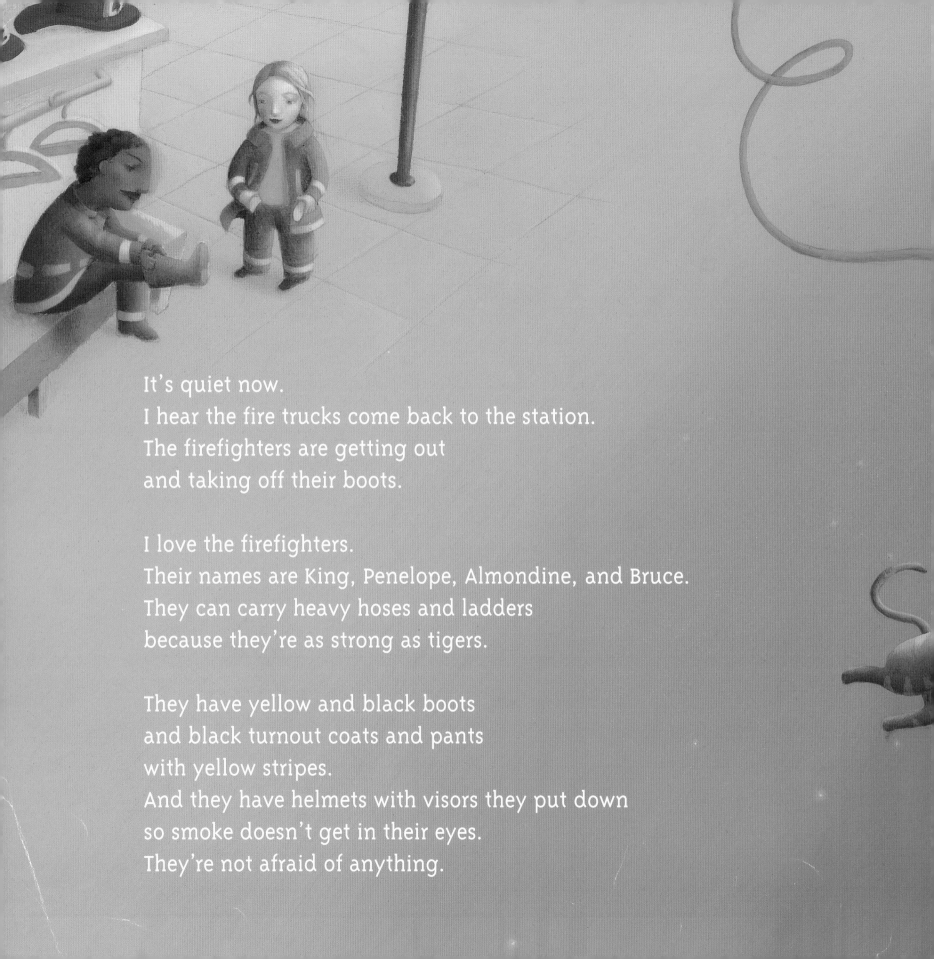

It's quiet now.
I hear the fire trucks come back to the station.
The firefighters are getting out
and taking off their boots.

I love the firefighters.
Their names are King, Penelope, Almondine, and Bruce.
They can carry heavy hoses and ladders
because they're as strong as tigers.

They have yellow and black boots
and black turnout coats and pants
with yellow stripes.
And they have helmets with visors they put down
so smoke doesn't get in their eyes.
They're not afraid of anything.

When they get back to the fire station,
they're very dirty from all the ash
and they have to take a bath.

But as soon as they're in their tubs, playing with the bubbles,
the alarm will ring again
and they'll have to slide down the fire pole, still wet from their bath!

Listen! Did you hear that?
I think I hear the sirens again, howling and howling.
The dog down the street is howling too.
The sirens sound far away this time —
that's because the fire is all the way in Mexico.

What happened was this:
There's a garden there full of chili peppers so hot
that when you take a bite, your mouth feels like it's on fire.
Well, there was a lady
in her garden, planting poppies,
and she felt a little hungry, so she nibbled on a pepper.
It was so hot, sparks flew from her tongue!

The firefighters have to come and spray her face with water.
Then they take their rakes and their shovels
and rake up all the burning embers that fell out of her mouth.

Those embers are fire-seeds,
and they grow into fire-flowers,
but the firefighters spray them with water until they disappear.
The lady's so grateful,
she gives them some poppies and zucchinis to take home.

Almondine loves zucchini, and Bruce likes bananas.
Penelope eats only peas, pasta, and pickles.
King likes vegetables, so he's really strong,
but toast is his favorite, with lots of jam.

They'll be having breakfast soon, after they sleep.
Maybe I'll go and visit them in the morning.
Once they gave me a hat and a sticky badge,
and King let me sit in the truck.

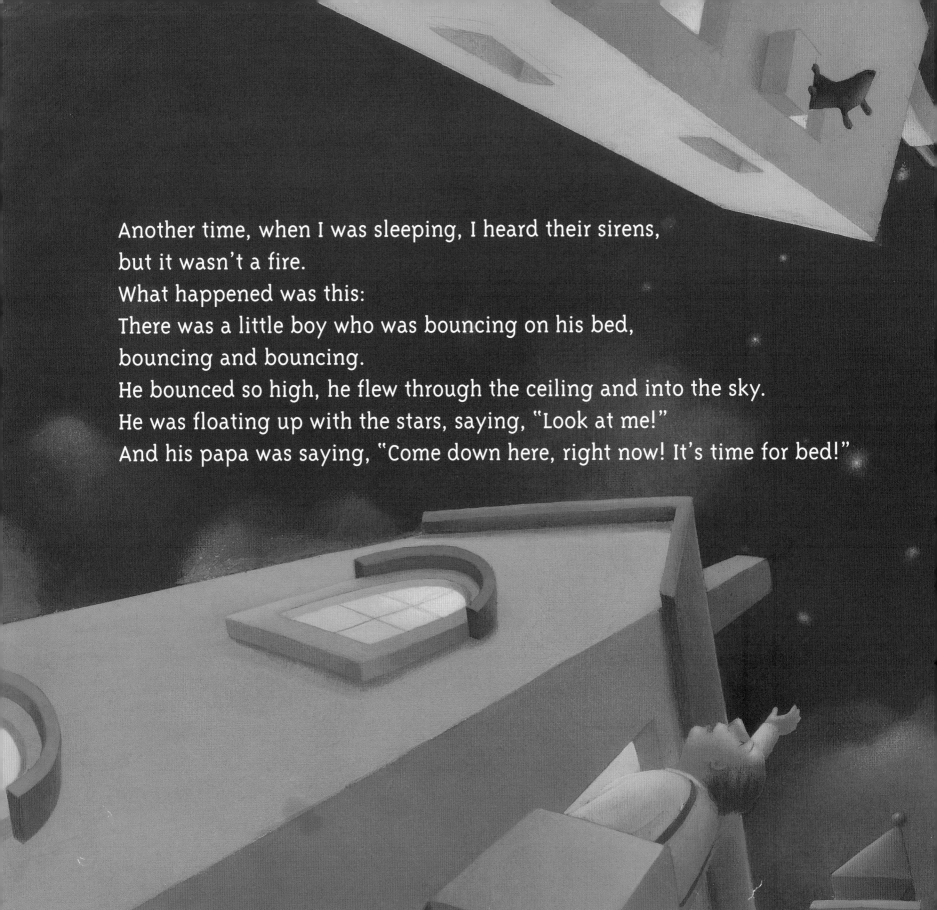

Another time, when I was sleeping, I heard their sirens,
but it wasn't a fire.
What happened was this:
There was a little boy who was bouncing on his bed,
bouncing and bouncing.
He bounced so high, he flew through the ceiling and into the sky.
He was floating up with the stars, saying, "Look at me!"
And his papa was saying, "Come down here, right now! It's time for bed!"

So the firefighters came with their aerial ladder truck.
The ladder went up and up,
past the moon and Mars and Venus,
up to Pluto, where the boy was floating.
The boy said, "Did you see how high I jumped?"
And Almondine said, "You can't be up on Pluto in pajamas—
you need a space suit and some mittens."
And so she carried him down the ladder and back to bed.

Sometimes at night, when I shut my eyes,
I can hear the fire engine outside my window.
Its motor goes *purr, purr* like a big red cat,
and King stretches the ladder to my bed.

"Come out," he says. "Come out and ride.
The stars are too hot tonight—we have to cool them down."

So we climb into the truck and drive into the sky—
me, King, Penelope, Almondine, and Bruce.
The clouds are full of water
and we put them in our hoses
and spray away the fire in the stars.

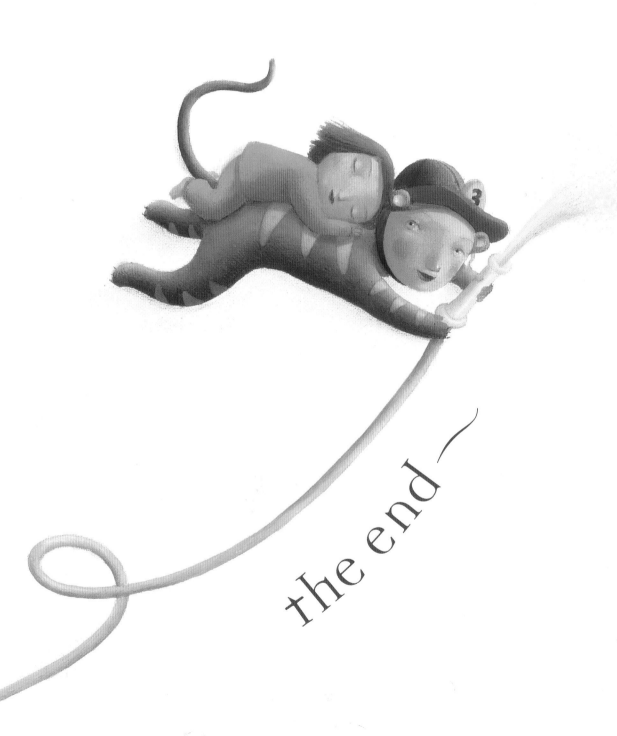

the end